Title: A Love Against All Odds
Subtitle: Vampire MF Romance Short Story

From the Author:
Thank you for purchasing this book.

Table of Contents

A Love Against All Odds
Description

Vampires have long taken over the human world since the reign of King Lucas Ice, who has ruled for two centuries.

He is ruthless and treats every human like dirt. He hates human with passion and hunts them at night for their blood.

He is every human's nightmare and at the same time, every lady's daydream.

Ariana Scott is just a small-town girl. Her world revolves around her ill father. She would do anything to save him even if it means bowing down to the vampires, the same kind who killed her mother.

King Lucas has gone centuries looking and waiting for his mate—his human mate. The same kind he hates.

All Lucas wants is blood and all Ariana wants is freedom.

Will the two unlikely pair ever learn to bow down to their fates? Will Lucas finally accept Ariana as his mate? Or does his hatred of human keep him away?

Chapter 1

Ariana had just finished her shift at the bakery and was walking down the narrow street that led to her house when she heard some rustling in the bushes.

She stopped in her tracks and held unto the cross around her neck. The cross was the only form of protection human had over vampires and still it never helped. She was just one of the few lucky ones who had never been bitten by a vampire.

The sound of approaching footsteps behind her brought her back to reality and she started to run clutching her bag to her chest.

She was suddenly blocked by a vampire who looked at her like she was his last meal.

"Henry, look what we have here," the vampire said as he looked behind her.

Despite her scared state, she looked behind her to see another vampire who was smiling at her.

Henry sniffed her neck making her shiver "mmm she smclls so sweet."

The other vampire's eyes flashed red and his fangs protruded as he pulled her closer to himself.

"Don't touch me," she yelled as she tried to wriggle out of his hold but his grip on her was strong.

"You are ours now sweetheart," he chuckled and bent toward her neck ready to drink her blood.

" Please don't," she pleaded amid tears.

It wasn't a full moon. Nor was it nine o'clock curfew. Human were not to be found outside past nine o'clock or else they would be feasted on by the vampires.

She had always followed that rule. She didn't know what she had done to deserve this. She obeyed the rules yet she was about to be feasted on by two smelly vampires.

By the look in their eyes, she knew she wasn't going to survive that night. She closed her eyes and prayed that her father would have the strength to bear his loss.

The pain never came.

"What is going on here?" a deep husky voice broke through her thoughts.

Lucas frowned on seeing two vampires surrounding a helpless woman. He was just having his normal walk round the city when he had heard a distant scream. He didn't know what took over him that he used his speed and followed her scream.

The two dirty looking vampires on recognizing him quickly bowed their heads in fear.

"Your Majesty." They echoed the greeting shivering in fear that they were caught breaking the rules.

The king is here! I'm surely going to die tonight, she thought to herself. Not daring to open her eyes to meet the King's.

"I asked you a question, what is going in here?!" he growled in anger.

"We were... We were just passing by and we-we saw her."

Lucas crossed his arms "You do know it's not yet nine o'clock, right? So why are you hell-bent on breaking the rules?"

"We just couldn't resist her scent, Your Majesty. We are sorry," Henry said bowing his head.

"Her scent?" Lucas frowned. He stared at the scared woman who had her eyes closed tightly in fear.

He got it now. Her scent was enticing and made him hungry but he always followed rules and he wasn't about to break them.

He turned to look at the two scared vampires "Let her go!" he commanded and they instantly released their hold on her making her stumble backward and fall.

She opened her eyes and yelped in pain as she gripped her wrist which had gotten bruised by the fall.

Lucas eyes flashed red at the careless vampires but he bit his lips to control his anger. He didn't know why he was feeling sorry for a human when he had done worse to their kind.

He glared at his men. "Let this be the last time you would do this or I will have you two killed."

He studied the two vampires for a moment before gesturing to them to leave. They ran away afraid that he would change his mind and kill them.

Ariana winced in pain feeling pains in her back and wrist due to the impact of the fall.

She made herself stand up in order to run away but strong hands held her up.

She looked up to behold her saviors' face only to meet the darkest eyes she had ever seen staring back at her. He looked so handsome that she doubted if he was real.

His eyes intrigued and scared her at the same time.

Sure that he was about to finish what his men started, she jolted away from him and started running for her dear life.

He laughed and ran after her blocking her way.

"I just saved you, woman."

"Please, let me go. I haven't done anything. I followed the rules," she pleaded desperate to be set free.

Her voice was soothing and her vanilla scent was invading his senses. He wanted to taste her and yet he couldn't.

He wanted to convince himself so badly that it was because of his obsession with rules but he knew damn well that he couldn't bear to hurt her to his dismay.

"Your Majesty," Jones, his right-hand man, yelled as he caught up with his king.

"We've been looking for you everywhere," Jones said but stopped upon seeing the girl.

"Who is she?" he asked Lucas who was still staring at the helpless woman.

"Leave," Lucas said to Ariana who looked dumbfounded.

"Get out of here before I change my mind!" he yelled at her causing her to flinch.

He needed her to leave for his own sanity. He didn't want his men to know that he had just saved a human.

She quickly picked up her bag and ran for her dear life not daring to look behind her.

On getting to her house, she quickly opened the door and locked it. She rested her back against the door and sank down, breathing heavily.

"That was so close."

"Ariana!" her father called as he limped toward her, worry lacing his features.

She quickly stood up and composed herself not wanting to worry her dad.

"Dad, how are you?"

"I'm fine but how are you?" He gave her a knowing look as if saying *I saw how distraught you looked.*

She faked a smile "I just had a bad day at the bakery, Dad. I'm fine."

He approached her limping but she ran to him and gave him his walking stick that was across the room.

"I already told you to quit the job."

"Dad, that's the only place that pays me a good salary and is nice to human. You know this already."

"But still, you are hardly at home because of it. I hardly see my daughter."

Her father's eyes were teary and she felt her heart break at the sight.

Her father was still in his late forties but looked like he was in his sixties. He had gotten frail and had lost all his will to live since her mother died ten years ago. She was caught outside during the full moon and the vampires drank her blood until there was none left.

She could still remember the pain in her father's eyes as he stared at her mother's lifeless body by the river.

He had only continued living because of her and she couldn't bring herself to tell him what happened that night.

It would only cause him more pain and he would forbid her from going out when they clearly needed the money.

She wrapped her hands around her dad. "I understand you Dad. I wish I could spend more time with you but you know we need the money for your medicine and our living expenses."

He nodded in understanding.

"Have you eaten because I brought some bread." She smiled excitedly at her father.

"I've already eaten. I was just waiting for you to come home."

"Well now I'm home, let's get you to bed."

She led her father to his room and helped him lie down on the shabby mattress.

She sighed in frustration as she glanced around the old shabby room. She wished she could get better jobs and renovate their house but it wasn't possible for her or any human either.

The vampires held the top positions while human slaved away for them and were paid and fed little. Anyone who protested met their death.

It was only the human that betrayed their race and supplied blood to the vampires that were treated better and had higher ranking.

The thought of what those heartless vampires almost did to her made her shudder and she walked out of her father's house.

She couldn't understand why the king let her go and she didn't want to know either. She just hoped that whatever reason it was, it wouldn't come back and bite her in the back.

That night, a man with dark eyes and golden hair invaded her dreams.

Chapter 2

It had been two days since Lucas had saved the beauty but for some reason he couldn't get her out of his head. The fact that she had invaded his dreams too was not helping matters.

Unable to stand it anymore, he had sent his men to bring her to his castle. He had a lot of questions waiting for her.

He needed to see her again. He needed to understand why he was so nice to her. He needed to know why her voice soothed him and why her blood was so enticing.

Just then Jones walked in and bowed to him.

"Your Majesty, we have brought the woman."

Lucas sat up on his throne on hearing the news.

"Bring her in," he ordered while Jones nodded and left.

He came back a moment later with two other guards who were holding the object of his dreams.

Her brunette hair cascaded down to her waist in contrast to that night when her hair was in a ponytail. She was dressed in a white top and faded jeans.

He could see the shock and fear in her eyes as she met his eyes. But the moment was broken when his men threw her to the floor.

Their actions were justified given that no human had the right to meet the King eyes except when he demanded them to. Yet he didn't understand why it pained him to see her hurt.

"You may look at me."

Ariana couldn't bring herself to look up fearing another punishment.

She was at her bakery when three vampires walked in and carried her against her will. She only recognized one of them from that night and that only confirmed her fears.

He left his throne in anger and walked toward her. He bent to her level and held her chin. His alluring scent invaded her senses.

"How dare you ignore me! Look at me!" he yelled while she slowly lifted her eyes to meet his.

Her emerald eyes held fear and he didn't like it. He didn't like that she feared him. He stepped away from her while she exhaled in relief.

"What is your name?"

"Ariana...Ariana Scott."

He watched as she gripped her shirt in fear avoiding his intense gaze on her.

"How old are you?"

"I'm nineteen, Your Majesty," she replied but couldn't help but wonder why he was asking all those questions.

"She's old enough, Your Majesty," Jones said.

Ariana couldn't help but blurt out, "Old enough for what?" she looked between the two men to see if she had missed something.

Lucas chuckled startling his men. He never laughed and hardly smiled. Thus, for a random human's words to earn that reaction from him made his men look at each other in surprise.

"My dear, did you really think I would just let you go just like that uhm?"

She shook her head.

She knew that letting her go was out of his character but she had hoped that it was her luck.

"You have to repay me for my kindness. I don't do things for free, little human." He smirked bending down to her level.

He held her chin and leaned closer to her, "You have to serve me as my maid."

Her heart sank as she processed his words.

Maid! Am I dreaming? That can't be possible, she thought to herself.

"Please, your majesty, I will do anything else but not that," she pleaded while he released her and stood up.

"You really have some guts to disobey me, Ariana."

For some reason, the way he said her name sent chills down her body. It was weird that she liked the way he said her name.

She bent her head "I'm sorry, your majesty. I wouldn't dare to disobey you. I just can't leave my ill father alone. I'm the only one he has."

Henry laughed mirthlessly throwing his head back. The girl really had some nerve.

He could easily have buried his fangs in her neck and drank her blood until she died. However, something stopped him no matter how much he craved her blood.

He glared at her. "It's not a choice. It's an order and if you really care about your father, you would not protest anymore."

He turned to look at Jones who was standing at a corner in the room with his two guards.

"Take her away," he ordered while the men took to action and carried her.

Ariana bit her lip to stop the looming tears. She wouldn't dare give him the satisfaction of seeing her tears.

The two guards dragged her down the stairs with Jones following behind them even though she wasn't putting up a fight.

The castle itself was dark and dangerous looking. It gave a feeling of power and at the same time loneliness which reflected in the king himself.

They stopped in front of a room down the hallway and Jones opened the door. Without warning, they threw her into the dungeon-looking room and locked her inside.

She looked around the cold dark room, thankful for the torch on the wall that aided her vision.

The room was small and couldn't contain more than four people with the small mattress in the room.

It looked more like a prison than a room and it made her shudder in fear to think that would be her life now.

She let out a loud cry. She was angry and frustrated at herself for being caught by the vampires. She was angry that she had to leave her poor father alone. She was angry at herself for thinking that the King was just being kind.

How wrong she was.

The door opened startling her and a young woman walked in.

The woman looked to be in her late twenties, her blonde hair was short and trimmed which made her look more mature. She was pretty and looked kind.

But one thing made Ariana glad, the woman did not have a red ring in her eyes which meant that she was not a vampire.

"You are quite pretty. I can see why he bent the rule for you."

The woman probably noticed her confused state and chuckled ."Pardon my manners. I'm Ciara, the head of the human maids."

She then handed Ariana a long black gown with puffy sleeves.

"What is this?" Ariana asked as she stared at the gown in her hands and Ciara simultaneously.

"King Lucas ordered that you wear this outfit and report to his chambers as soon as possible."

Ciara held her hand out for Ariana to take and she obliged.

"I can see and understand the fear in your eyes. I have been in your shoes before and I can tell you it has not been a pretty good experience. I'm just one of the lucky few that is still alive."

"How long have you been here?"

Ciara sighed before she replied "Four years, I've been in this hell for four years."

Ariana bit her lip. "I'm sorry."

Ciara smiled, pleased at the girl's innocence "You know since I've been working here, the king has never had a personal maid. He never liked someone breaching his privacy, especially a human. Everyone is eager to meet you, you know."

"Can we still visit our families while we are here?" Ariana asked the question that had been bugging her mind since. She could care less about the king.

Ciara shook her head "He's our family now. You can't leave the four walls of the castle anymore. Your life starts and ends here."

"I will wait for you outside while you change. Mind you, the king gave us ten minutes, I would be quick if I were you."

She smiled and left the room.

Ariana wiped her cheeks and sighed in defeat. She still cherished her life. She had to keep on living for her father's sake.

She quickly stripped off her clothes and wore the dress. The dress was floor length and almost covered her toes. It fitted her perfectly and pushed up her bust, showing a little bit of cleavage.

She was glad that it wasn't short at least even though she was uncomfortable showing her cleavage.

She opened the door and met eyes with Ciara who was leaning against the wall.

"You look beautiful," she commented staring at Ariana as if she was some princess.

No one had her called her beautiful except her father and her best friend Tommy. She wondered if they were already looking for her though she knew it wasn't past her closing time at the bakery.

"Thanks though, I feel like I'm going to trip in the dress."

Ciara chuckled and shrugged "You will do just fine."

Ciara started to walk down the dark dungeon until she reached a door and opened it.

"Come." She gestured to Ariana to follow her and the latter obliged.

They walked into a large golden hall, a different part of the castle that looked more beautiful than the other side.

"This is where the important maids and guards lives," Ciara said while Ariana stared at the large room with different compartments in wonder.

Several vampires looked at them as they passed making Ariana feel uneasy and walk closely with Ciara, afraid that one of the vampires would pounce on her at any given opportunity.

They climbed up a set of stairs before they stopped before a huge door.

"This is the King's chambers."

Ariana felt her heart race at the revelation. She wasn't ready to face the king yet.

Ciara opened the huge iron door to reveal a large hallway.

Ciara pushed Ariana into the room, gave her a thumbs up and shut the door behind her, startling Ariana.

She took a deep breath and looked around the hallway until her eyes landed on the king.

He was seated on his golden throne with a golden crown on his head.

She finally noticed what he was wearing. His black shirt hugged his muscles perfectly matched with black jeans and golden shoes.

He looked ethereal. To say he was good-looking was an understatement. His whole form emitted power and danger.

It didn't help matters that his eyes were burning into hers. She quickly looked away unable to stand his intimidating eyes and the fact that it made her heart race.

Lucas swept his eyes down her form. She looked so beautiful in the dress he picked for her. It hugged her curves perfectly and her bust.

He felt his groin tightening and laughed so hard, he could feel tears in his eyes.

He could see the confusion in her eyes but she still didn't look at him.

His blood was rushing hot and to the wrong places.

He had definitely lost his mind. He actually had a boner for a human, a woman who was completely covered. He was insane.

He was dying to touch her, to sink his fangs in her neck and drink her blood.

He wanted his breath all over her. He wanted a lot of things and it scared him.

He wasn't a fool. He knew what this all meant. He had always wanted a mate. He had gone centuries looking and waiting for that special someone who would make his heart rate.

It angered him that a human had made him feel like that.

Why couldn't she be a vampire? he thought to himself.

He needed to stay away from her for his own sanity. He didn't have any need for a human mate. She was forbidden and it had to remain that way.

"Leave," he ordered breaking the silence in the room.

She flinched at the sound of his voice and finally looked up to meet his eyes.

"I said leave!" he yelled once again and she quickly turned away from him and walked out while he eased a sigh of relief.

He needed a breather and most definitely a cold shower.

Chapter 3

It had been a day since her stay in the castle and all Ariana wanted was a chance to escape.

After the king ordered her to leave, she was assigned the toughest of jobs by Jones. She spent that whole day gardening, washing the plates used by over a hundred servants and then cleaned the dungeon.

She had felt numb and weak and was fed a measly porridge.

She had been told by Ciara that the king was the one who ordered Jones to make her life a living hell

She wondered what she had done wrong to infuriate him as she folded the last of his clothes and placed them on top of his other clothes on the table

Just then Jones barged into the laundry room startling her.

"The king wants you in his room now!"

She quickly wiped her hands with a towel. Knowing better than to hesitate, she followed Jones out of the laundry room.

Lucas gulped the last of his brandy and placed the bottle on the table. He had just sent Amelia, his mistress out of the room after her several attempts to seduce him proved futile.

Usually he would have succumbed but he couldn't bring himself to sleep with her for fear that he would call Ariana's name in the throes of passion.

He wondered when it had gotten so bad to that extent. Staying away from Ariana was not helping him in any way. It only made him angry and frustrated as he yearned for her even more.

A knock came on his bedroom door jolting him out of his thoughts.

"Your Majesty, it's Jones. I've brought Ariana."

A smile played on Lucas lips at the mention of her name and he replied, "Let her in."

The door opened and Ariana stepped in while Jones closed the door after her and left.

Her eyes scanned the large room which was beautifully decorated with elegance that exuded royalty.

Her eyes landed on Lucas who was seated on his bed watching her. He was dressed in a white robe and his hair was wet and messy with a few strands falling over his face but he still looked handsome.

It was then it dawned on her that she was alone in his room, at his mercy.

Fear gripped her heart as he stared her down making her uncomfortable. She gripped her long lavender gown happy that it covered her up completely.

"Sit." He pointed to a chair in the corner of the room that had a large table in front of it.

She gathered up her gown and made her way to the chair and sat on it.

"Take the book and read to me." He pointed to an old book on the table which had torn covers.

Her hand shook as she carried the book and opened the first page.

"Once upon a time, there was a vampire who was lonely and cold. He had spent years waiting for the special mate who would keep him warm and complete."

She pursed and looked up to meet his eyes watching her.

He frowned

"Did I tell you to stop?"

She shook her head and continued reading. "One day he saw a little young woman by the riverside playing with her puppy and asked her for water. The young woman, to his surprise, didn't judge his shabby look and used her bottle to fetch the water and handed it to him."

"Do you think vampires have an iota of kindness within them?" Lucas asked as he gauged her reaction.

She looked up to meet his eyes which was watching her intensely "I don't think they do."

He smiled and crossed his arms and leaned his head against the headboard. "Why do you think so?"

She gave him an incredulous look. "vampires are heartless and could care less about human. You torture us for your own pleasure and love watching us cower in pain and shame."

She was surprised that she had said those words but she didn't regret them. She was angry, hungry, tired and missed her father. Yet the king was in the comfort of his own home enjoying himself while she suffered for no reason at all.

"I appreciate your honesty."

Her stomach grumbled breaking the silence and she blushed while he smiled amused.

"Do you believe in love, Ariana and why?"

"I do. Even though I was a little child, I witnessed the longing looks my parents gave each other. They were in love and that love has continued even in death."

He could see the tears glistening in her eyes as she remembered her parents. His heart melted.

He cleared his throat and sat up on the bed.

"Do you think a vampire could ever love a human?" The way, he was staring at her as if daring her to say the wrong thing.

"I find it absurd given that both races hate each other and nothing good can ever come out of such a union."

It was true. It was forbidden and a great betrayal when a vampire and human mated. It was wrong and the ones who indulged in such acts were seen as outcasts who sold out their race. She could never understand that kind of love.

He felt his heart break at her answer. He didn't know why and he didn't need to know why. She had pushed the wrong buttons and he didn't know what to do to her.

"Get me dinner in the next five minutes," he ordered her and she quickly jolted up at the sound of his voice and bolted out of his room.

It took her two minutes to get to the kitchen, with another two minutes to get dinner.

It finally took her three minutes to bring his dinner to the room and with the way he was glaring at her. She knew she was dead meat.

It wasn't her fault that his room was so far from the kitchen. She had tried her best to meet up with his time by running but it hadn't been enough.

She just couldn't understand why he had asked her to get his dinner when he had already eaten.

Despite the exhaustion, she forced a smile and placed his dinner on the table in front of him.

"Here you go, sir," she said.

He smiled and instead on digging in, he said "Eat, it's yours."

"What?!" She couldn't have heard him right.

"I've already eaten. Eat it, it's yours."

He looked serious and wasn't going to take no for an answer.

She reluctantly sat in front of him, feeling uncomfortable that she was so close to him.

She took her fork and twirled the pasta. She brought the food to her lips and ate it.

It tasted so delicious that she couldn't help but moan. She had never had pasta before but she had seen it in books and couldn't believe that she was actually eating it.

She thought back to her father, knowing fully well that he would love to eat it too.

She bit her lip to prevent herself from getting emotional and continued eating the food oblivious to the reaction her moan had caused.

Lucas watched her in amazement. He loved the sound of her moan and it made him think of how much he would love her to sound like that when she was under him.

He closed his eyes to will the thought away. He was getting hard for a human and it was unheard of. Even her scent was pulling him in.

"Your majesty, I'm done," She announced as she wiped her mouth with the handkerchief.

He opened his eyes and it landed on her moist lips. They was so inviting and he knew he was going to regret his next action but his self-control was out the window.

Before he knew it, he was resting his hands on either side of her chair while she stared at him in fear. Her heart thumping against her chest and her breath hitched due to the proximity.

"Your majesty?" Her voice came out as a croak.

His gaze was intimidating and it seemed his eyes pierced through hers in a mysterious way.

He grabbed her neck and his lips met hers. She felt strange tingles on her body. His soft lips caressed her upper lip gently and she didn't know when she gave in and moved her lips and tongue with his.

He felt so high on tasting her lips and lost it and deepened the kiss as if his life depended on it.

She felt giddy as he deepened the kiss.

He only pulled out of the kiss because he was out of breath. They both gasped for air while the reality of what they had just done dawned on them.

He stood up and started pacing the room. He felt disgusted with himself for his lack of self-control.

He turned to look at her. Her lips were swollen and it only made him yearn to taste her more.

"Get out!" he yelled startling her.

She jolted up from her seat and ran out of the room, ashamed that she had enjoyed the kiss and entertained it.

Chapter 4

It had been a week since the kiss. What Ariana wanted to do was forget about it but it seemed impossible.

She still remembered how high she felt when she kissed him. It was a pleasant and scary feeling at the same time.

He had stolen her first kiss and for some reason she was glad he was her first.

She hadn't seen the king since then. He had embarked on a trip the next day although she was still assigned to clean his room.

She had just finished mopping the hall way when she felt someone watching her.

She turned to look behind her only to receive the shock of her life.

Tommy, her best friend was standing beside a Pillar watching her.

"Tommy?" she called unsure.

He nodded and ran toward her enveloping her in a hug. She returned the hug feeling happy that she was seeing her friend again.

"I've missed you so much," Tommy said as he pulled out of the hug to behold her face.

"I've missed you too," Ariana replied sad and happy at the same time before reality dawned on her "What are you doing here?"

Tommy rubbed the back of his neck. "I work here now."

"What! Are you insane?" She couldn't help but express her shock that Tommy was actually working in the castle.

"I'm not. I applied to work here because of you. Your dad was worried sick about you especially when he found out that you were working here."

The mention of her dad made her sad. "How is he?"

"He's fine. He is actually being taken care of by two nurses."

"You hired them?"

Tommy shook his head. "No, I wish I did though but it wasn't me. They are from the palace."

She opened her mouth in shock. It wasn't possible. The king was heartless and he had forbidden her from visiting her father. There was no way he could be responsible for that.

"The palace? When did that happen?"

"Since the day you left. The king sent two nurses to take care of your dad. They even redecorated your house."

The king had a heart after all.

"I just couldn't sit by and worry about your welfare when I could just be beside you."

"But you know how dangerous this place is for humans. You can't work here, Tommy."

"What makes you say that? You look perfectly fine." He looked confused and examined her as if to see if she were hurt anywhere.

"Why were you brought here?" he asked.

"I was brought here to repay a favor," she simply answered. It sounded inadequate to her as well. She really didn't know of what use she was to the king.

"Hey, you two get back to work," yelled one of the guards at the corner of the hallway.

"I'll see you later," she muttered to Tommy who nodded and left for his post.

She carried her cleaning materials and headed for the king's room.

She opened the door and gasped in shock to see the king seated in his favorite chair across the room.

He looked as handsome as ever with his blond hair glowing in the room.

"It took you long enough."

When had he returned that she didn't notice? Maybe, because she was caught up with her conversation with Tommy, that's why.

He stood up from his seat and walked toward her.

Her heart rate quickened and she could feel her palms get sweaty when he stopped in front of her.

"I can smell a manly scent in you. Who the fuck were you with?" he asked.

His question caught her off guard and her lips slightly parted.

"I was with a dear friend of mine," she answered honestly confused as to why he was so interested in that.

His eyes changed colors, going from black to red. He was losing his temper and it was frightening.

He grabbed a hold of her arm "I was gone a week and you've jumped into another man's arms already."

His grip tightened around her arms and she winced in pain but he couldn't care less.

"Please let me go. You're hurting me," she pleaded but her pleas were ignored.

"Who is he to you?" he growled.

The pain in her arms was enough to render her dumb but she replied anyway.

"He's my best friend."

He scoffed and pushed her against the wall making her feel a searing pain in her back but he wasn't done yet.

"Do you love him?" His voice was low and dangerous at the same time.

She couldn't bring herself to say anything anymore since it seemed like no matter what she said, he was hell bent on hurting her.

"I can clearly see that you love him. Your eyes gave you away."

"Wha-what have I done wrong?" she asked.

He closed the space between them, still gripping her hand harshly. "You invaded my dreams, made me restless. To top it all up, you allowed another person to touch you, hold you."

The way he said it sounded as if he was in pain which baffled her.

He released her hand and she sank to the floor holding her arm which now had red finger marks on them.

He knelt down before her and his eyes swept over her form. He grabbed her neck and pulled her closer to him.

"It's time you learn that you are mine, mate."

Before she could process what he meant, he had sank his fangs into the flesh of her neck.

He held her down by the shoulders preventing her from squirming.

Her blood tasted sweeter than he had ever imagined and he couldn't get enough. She tasted so right for him quenching his thirst.

He moaned at her sweetness, completely mesmerized by the taste of her

She screamed and tried to push him away but it only urged him further. Tears streamed down her face as the pain coursed through her body.

She felt numb, weak and tired. Black spots appeared in her vision and everything seemed to darken around her. Before she knew it, she had blacked out.

******

She slowly opened her eyes to adjust to the lighting in the room. It took her a moment to recognize her surroundings. She was lying down on the king's bed.

She jolted up only to see that the king was seated in front of her.

Her arms and neck arched so badly that she almost wished that she had died instead.

"Finally, you are awake," he sarcastically said.

He stood up from his chair and buried his hands in his pants' pockets.

"By the way I've dealt with your lover boy."

Her ears picked up at that "What did you do to him?"

He smiled "Let's just say he won't be anywhere near you again." "What the hell did you do to him?" She hoped Tommy was okay. She wouldn't be able to forgive herself if something bad happened to him.

Lucas eyes narrowed. "I don't appreciate the tone of your voice, Ariana."

She was terribly wrong to have thought he was kind. He was proving her wrong day after day.

"Let him go. He didn't do anything wrong. You are sick," she yelled at him while he stared at her in surprise.

He laughed mirthlessly. "Yes, you are right. I am sick. Sick in the head to feel this way about you—a worthless human."

He traced his fingers on her neck where he bit her. She flinched away from him.

"You are now mine and mine only. No one else can claim you, not even that fat headed rascal."

"His name is Tommy and nothing is going on between us. The fact that your lonely ass doesn't know what friendship entails is not my fault."

He pushed her down the bed. Her head fell back into a mass of pillows and he climbed on top of her.

The fear of what he was about to do to her made her voice break "Please don't."

It amazed him how she moved from strong to helpless in minutes.

He held her down by her shoulders and buried his face in her neck.

She feared that he was going to drink from her again. She wasn't sure if she could survive another one.

She started to squirm under him, trying as much as possible to get him to leave her alone.

He raised his head and glared at her "If you don't stop moving, I'm going to do something we would both regret."

She stopped knowing fully well that he would make good on his threat.

He licked her wound. At first she felt the pain as he licked it but later felt no pain at all.

He climbed off her "The maid would soon be here to get you ready for your new job," he simply said. Not giving her a second glance he stepped out of the room.

What kind of job was he talking about, has he gone insane? she thought to herself.

A few moments later, the door opened and four maids entered followed by Ciara carrying different clothes.

"Ciara," Ariana exclaimed in joy as she sprang out of bed and embraced the woman. She had missed Ciara even though they had only known each other recently.

Ciara was the only human maid who interacted with her and shared her pain. The other girls saw her as a competition. As if she wished the king's attention upon herself.

She pulled out of the hug to behold Ariana's face.

"What is my job now?"

Ciara seemed to hesitate for a moment before she answered. "You are now his mistress."

"What is a mistress?" she asked.

"It's the highest position a human can hold here and you are the first human the king has chosen."

Ciara stared to gauge Ariana's reaction before she continued.

"Your body and blood is to satisfy him and him alone."

She couldn't have heard Ciara right.

"What did you say?"

"You clearly heard me, Ariana. Don't make it hard for yourself and everyone else here. If you value your life, you will obey him."

She couldn't believe that Ciara was making it seem like it was no big deal at all. It was a big deal to her or any normal human out there. Her life had practically changed in the course of two weeks and another bomb was just dropped on her.

"He would have to kill me first before he can have me."

She could see the shocked expressions on the maids' faces while Ciara stood stoic.

"Go and prepare the bath for our lady," Ciara ordered the maids who eagerly left for the bathroom. They obviously were too afraid and shocked by Ariana's words.

"If you don't value your life, I value mine. No one dares to disobey the king's orders. Just because he has been nice to you doesn't mean he can't be cruel."

"Nice?" Ariana scoffed, "He has been cruel to me from the very start. Why are you so distant all of a sudden?"

Ciara sighed. "I'm not supposed to talk to you at all. I'm just supposed to prepare you for him. There's a lot of confusion in the palace right now. Rumors are swirling around that you are the king's mate and that he's in love with you."

Ariana couldn't believe her ears. "In love? He isn't capable of loving anyone."

"That's what we thought too but since you've been working here. He has been incredibly nice and smiles a lot more. He hasn't gone on his hunting spree for a while now, which is unusual."

She paused for a moment and examined Ariana's neck "Has he drank from you?"

Ariana nodded.

"There's no mark?" Ciara frowned as she checked for any marks but found none before she took a step back.

"See, he healed you. Vampires don't heal humans. They prefer that they die or writhe in pain. Vampires only heal their human mates."

"What the hell is a mate?" Ariana asked the question that had been bugging her mind since.

"A mate is like your other half. They complete you. You can't help but feel drawn to them. You won't be able to control your feelings around them, whenever they touch you,

you will feel a spark of electricity. You get very possessive and aggressive when you see your mate in another's arms. It is the strongest and everlasting form of love in the entire universe."

"Do you have a mate?"

Ciara shook her head "I don't...I don't know. It's a very rare case for a human to have a mate. The only time that happens is when a vampire and a human are tied by fate."

"So you think that I'm the king's mate?"

"It's the only possible explanation for why he is bending so many rules for you."

Then she remembered his words,

"It's time you learn that you are mine, mate."

Chapter 5

Lucas entered his room and his eyes landed on the beauty who was seated on his chair reading his book.

She was clad in a short black night gown that didn't reach her knees showing off her smooth legs. He knew the idea of the dress was to please him and pleased he was.

The dress fitted her perfectly showcasing her curves and exposing her fair skin, it made him yearn to touch her.

He cleared his throat and she quickly looked up to see him. Her eyes widened and she quickly pulled down her dress feeling bare under his gaze.

There she was at his service. She was his and he was done fighting his feelings.

He had left the palace after the kiss they shared on the pretense of a business trip when in fact he was having a hard time dealing with his feelings for her.

He thought time away from her would clear his head but he was so wrong. It just made him yearn for her even more. Many women threw themselves at him but he couldn't bring himself to sleep with them or drink their blood.

He had come back to confess his feelings to her and apologize when he smelled a manly scent on her that sent his senses into overdrive.

He couldn't bear the fact that she was in love with someone else. It pained him to the core and he had that bastard locked up. He did regret venting his anger on her and tasting her blood until she collapsed.

That was very cruel of him. He had lost all self-control and having her so close by and smelling her lovely scent was hard to resist. Just like now when her vanilla scent filled the air.

He had it bad for Ariana and all he wanted was to mate her and mark her as his.

"You look ravishing."

Her eyes widened for the second time that evening and he was enjoying the effect that he had on her.

He sat on a chair in the corner of the room. "Come and sit." He patted his lap.

Her eyes travelled down to his lap and snapped up to meet his eyes.

"I would rather sit here, your majesty," she replied.

"If you really want your lover boy to live, sit." He watched as her mouth opened in shock and how his words worked magic.

He didn't mean to scare her. He just knew that would make her obey him.

She stood up and placed the book on the table.

"Bring the book with you and read to me."

She obeyed and picked up the book. She took small steps toward him as if approaching her doom, all the while avoiding looking at his eyes.

His scent was alluring and invaded her senses.

She slowly sat down on his lap but he pulled her closer by the waist so she was leaning against his chest.

Her breath hitched at the unexpected proximity. She expected him to release his hand from her waist but he kept it there.

She felt his breath on her neck. "Read to me," he demanded.

She quickly opened the book but before she could even utter a word, he had nuzzled her neck causing her to moan at the unexpected sensation.

"Your-your majesty?" she managed to mutter ignoring how right he felt against her.

"Shh- It's Lucas for you, my love," he whispered against her neck and she shivered.

She felt dizzy feeling things she had never felt before.

He sucked gently on her neck making sure that he didn't bite her. He couldn't bear her being in pain. He would only bite her if she wanted him to no matter how much he desired it.

He placed gentle kisses on her neck and she closed her eyes relishing in the feeling.

Her eyes fluttered open when he withdrew from her neck. She frowned for having lost contact with his warm lips.

"Stand up," he ordered.

He was back to his bipolar self. He would be nice to her for a moment and then push her away a moment later. She felt sick for having fallen for his tricks once again.

She stood up and clutched the book to her chest.

Lucas smiled and stood in front of her. She wouldn't meet his eyes so he lifted her chin making her look at him.

He gently pushed her against the wall and she was trapped.

His dark eyes sparkled with longing.

"You are mine, Ariana."

He kissed her softly and she kissed him back wrapping her arms round his neck.

His lips felt so warm and soft against hers. Their tongues moved in synchronization. It was a thrilling experience for both of them.

For Lucas, no kiss had ever felt like this for him. He was drunk on her taste and he kissed her as if he was afraid to let her slip away.

For Ariana, it was a strange but euphoric experience. The way he kissed her sent shivers down her spine. He tasted so familiar, so much like home, like he was made for her. She didn't want to let go.

Then a loud knock came at the door making Lucas to whine against her lips. The incessant knocking made him pull away from her.

She remained by the wall, her eyes slightly wide and her lips swollen with smudged lipstick on them. It was such an erotic sight that made him want to kiss her again. He moved forward to kiss her again but another loud knock landed on the door.

"Fuck!" he cursed and turned his gaze away from her.

He quickly opened the door and Jones walked in eager to deliver a news but stopped on noticing the tense atmosphere.

He quickly lowered his head, a knowing smile on his cheeks. "I'm sorry, your majesty."

"What you want to tell me better be worthwhile or I will have your head taken off your body," Lucas warned.

He was furious that his intimate moment with Ariana had been disrupted. It seemed like the universe was ganging up against him.

"I brought Mr. Scott over as you wanted, your majesty."

Lucas brushed his hand through his hair and nodded in understanding. He had asked Jones to bring Ariana's father to the palace. He knew it would make her happy and as he watched her connect the dots he smiled.

"My father?" she asked, hoping in her heart that it was true.

Lucas nodded and she enveloped him in a hug that almost made him fall. He wrapped his hands round her relishing in her body warmth.

"Thank you so much," she muttered against his neck and he stiffened. It was then she realized their awkward position and how it would have looked to Jones.

She jumped away from him mentally beating herself up for being embarrassing.

She bowed her head. "I'm sorry, your majesty," she apologized.

His thumb traced her swollen lips while her breath hitched. "Never apologize for touching me. I'm yours, my lady."

Jones stared at his master in wonder. He had noticed the positive changes in his master since Ariana stepped into the palace. He was no longer cruel and didn't bed random female vampires any more. He had surely found his mate.

He looked at Jones afraid that if he stared at Ariana the more, he was going to lose his self-control.

"Take her to her dad," He ordered while Jones nodded and left the room with Ariana following closely behind him.

Lucas plopped down on his bed and sighed. He was head over heels for a human. Being mates with a human didn't sound so bad after all.

******

She entered a large bedroom that Jones had opened for her.

"Dad?" she called on seeing her dad standing by the window side.

She ran toward him and embraced him.

"Ariana, my precious daughter, you don't know how much I've missed you."

"I've missed you too, Dad."

They both sat on the bed with Ariana placing her head on her father's shoulder.

"What did that bastard want from you that he brought you here?" She knew her father was referring to Lucas and it hurt her.

She sat up and looked at her worried dad. "He's not a bad man Dad. In fact I heard he's the one who hired nurses to take care of you."

"I never asked for that. Moreover these vampires don't do things for free. I'm sure he wants something in return."

"Dad, don't be ungrateful. He even brought you here to come and see me."

"Why are you defending a vampire? Have you forgotten that his kind is responsible for your mother's death?"

"I know but he wasn't at fault. Those vampires broke the rules and my dear mother paid for it. He is not a bad man, Papa. He actually saved me from bad vampires. If not, I wouldn't be here."

Her dad frowned. "You defend him so much as if he's you know him."

"Because I do, Papa. He's been nothing but nice to me."

Her father narrowed his eyes at her and asked the gnawing question "Who is he to you?"

The question rendered her speechless. Who was she to him? They had kissed twice and he had made her his mistress, called her his mate but she was still confused and scared.

What if he woke up one day and decided he didn't want her anymore. Every time he closed the gap between them, he stepped back creating an even greater gap.

He had called her *his* and she had felt it when he held her and kissed her senseless. She was his mate and he was hers. She was just not sure if he was ready to accept her and if she was ready to accept his feelings.

How could she break the news to her father that she had betrayed their race? How could she tell him that she was such a hypocrite, who hated hybrids but was on the verge of creating one?

"He is just my king," she answered truthfully. He was her king, her king in every way. He had stolen her heart since the first day she had seen him.

Chapter 6

Ariana stirred awake a few hours later and tried to make sense of her surroundings. Her head ached as her eyes couldn't make out where she was because the room was so dark.

The only thing she remembered was taking a walk in the garden earlier in the day and then someone popped up from behind her and covered her mouth with a white cloth and then she blacked out.

Her hands and legs were tied up so tightly she felt the rope sink in her skin.

She wondered who had kidnapped her.

She almost went to sleep when a door opened and the sound of footsteps approached her.

Someone switched on the light and she squinted her eyes to adjust to the lighting.

"Well, well, well, the little princess is awake," A female vampire said as she stood towering over Ariana with three men behind her.

She was gorgeous and had sparkly blue eyes with a red ring around it.

Was this woman her kidnapper?

"You see, little girl, I didn't want to hurt you at first because I thought that you were his next play thing but I thought wrong. He discarded me for you."

She let out a guttural laugh that startled Ariana who had no idea what she was talking about.

The woman must have noticed her confusion so she bent down to Ariana's level "I'm Amelia, the King's favorite mistress. I had no problem sharing him with others until you came. He basically dethroned me and shoved me way like trash just because of you."

"How is that my fault?"

Amelia sadistically laughed and slid down to her knees. She parted Ariana's hair in an almost motherly way "Oh little one, it's your fault."

She sniffed Ariana's neck and smiled "He has not mated with you because you don't smell like him. Thus, you are not his yet which makes my plan easier to execute."

"What are you going to do to me?" Ariana couldn't help but ask.

She stood up and glared at Ariana "This is your new home. You will live here until werewolves tear you apart. No one not even Lucas would be able to save you. I would be his shoulder to cry on then and you will just be a distant memory."

She started laughing uncontrollably angering Ariana who shouted at her. "You can do whatever you want to me but he would never love you. I will forever be his mate and no one would be able to take my place."

A hot slap landed on her face that almost rendered her deaf.

Amelia clutched the hand she had used to slap Ariana. "You made me hurt you. I didn't want to."

"Whether you are his mate or not doesn't matter to me, What matters is that I will be the one to warm his bed for all eternity while you rot in hell."

She laughed once again and gestured to her men to follow her. "Goodbye forever, Ariana."

Her voice echoed behind her while hot tears streamed down Ariana's face.

They left the door ajar and she could see that it was evening time. She could see the trees and the bushes before her and she knew she was done for.

She was in the forest. There was no way someone could find her.

Soon she heard the sounds of distant wear wolves.

"Help me, Lucas," she muttered. Hoping, praying that he heard her cries and would come and save her.

******

To say Lucas was furious was an understatement. He had been busy all day discussing how to reach an alliance with werewolves when Jones had barged in and declared Ariana missing.

He had dumped everything and now he was walking down the narrow bushes following her scent with his men following closely behind him.

He vowed to deal mercilessly with his men for letting his beloved be captured.

"Your highness, are you sure we are walking down the right path?" Jones asked as they brushed through the bushes.

"I'm the only one who can pick up her scent. So shut up and follow me." He rolled his eyes and continued to brush past the bushes following the faint smell of his beloved.

"Hang in there, my love," he muttered to himself.

He stopped beside an uncompleted building.

"What's wrong, your majesty?" Jones asked.

"She's here. I can smell her strongly here." He didn't wait for his men. He simply used his speed and ended up in the front of the building.

Inside the building lay his beloved. Her head was bent on her legs while her hands and legs were tied up.

His heart ached at the sight and he rushed to her and shook her awake.

"Ariana," he called as she stirred awake.

Her eyes opened and she gasped on seeing Lucas.

"Lucas!" she cried out in disbelief.

"It's me. You are safe now. I'm so sorry."

He loosened the rope on her arms and legs and she sighed in relief, happy that she was free.

"I won't let anyone take you away from me ever again."

Chapter 7

It had been a month since she had been captured and saved by Lucas and yet he couldn't shake the fear of her being taken away from him again.

He had increased her security and forbidden her from going outside without his company.

He had fed Amelia and her men to the werewolves as a lesson to anyone who dared to hurt his mate.

Everything was going great between him and Ariana. She had gotten used to his kisses and hugs. She was even sleeping next to him just like now that they were lying on his bed with her head on his naked chest.

"Lucas," she called as she looked at him while he looked down at her smiling.

"Yes." It felt amazing to hear her sweet voice as she cuddled against him.

"What is the process of mating?"

She felt his heart rate increase at her question and he cleared his throat "Why did you ask that question, Ariana?"

She shrugged. "It's just...Amelia told me she could hurt me because I wasn't yours yet."

He bit his lips at the mention of the witch's name. Amelia had been his main fuck buddy because of her alluring body but she was nothing compared to his mate. He only used Amelia to satisfy his thirst for his mate until he met Ariana.

He sat up and leaned his head against the head board while Ariana sat up too, watching him.

"I will have to make love to you, then give you my mark which would stop your aging process. That way you will never leave me and I would be able to protect you. We would also be able to feel each other's emotions," he explained while she blushed.

She closed the gap between them and kissed his cheek causing him to shiver. "Make love to me, Lucas."

The way she said his name was sensual.

He pulled away from her and narrowed his eyebrows. He couldn't have heard her right.

"What did you say?"

"I want you to make me yours," she said firmly.

He shook his head. "You don't know what you are saying."

She pouted. "I do. I've thought about it all month and I want it. I'm ready," she whined.

"Are you sure?"

"I've never been more sure in my entire life."

She didn't know where the confidence to tell him that had come from, but she didn't regret it. Over the past month, Lucas had changed his attitude toward humans.

He had released Tommy and promoted him to a high ranking official in the palace. Her father was also living in the palace and there were no longer human slaves.

Laws were made to make sure that humans were treated fairly. Although, every human had to donate their blood once every month to the vampires.

She understood why he couldn't share his powers with humans because they would betray him.

Over the past month, she had seen a lovely side to the dangerous man she once knew. She was now ready to become his, totally and completely.

He placed her down on the bed and climbed on top of her.

He kissed her hungrily as if he had been yearning for her for years. He sucked her lower lip and teasing nibbled on it which made her open her mouth and he slipped his tongue in. She tasted so delicious and inviting.

As he kissed her senseless, his hand traced down her neck to the inside of her night gown and cupped her right breast. He gently fondled it and pinched it.

She moaned at the unexpected pain mixed with pleasure that she felt.

He stopped kissing her and pulled back a little.

He released his hand from her breast and helped her remove her night gown leaving her in only her pink panties.

She felt exposed and tried to cover her breast with her hand but he caught her hand and shook his head disapprovingly.

"Don't. You look beautiful."

And she believed him especially with the way he looked at her with a longing glitter in his eyes.

He sucked her left breast before releasing it with a soft nibble and moving to the next mound repeating the same.

By now she was a moaning mess so lost in her pleasure that she didn't notice when he had spread her legs apart until he rubbed her through her panties.

"Please," she pleaded. She didn't know what she was pleading for but she just wanted him to do anything to complete the pleasure she was feeling.

He slowly and expertly pulled down her panties until she was completely naked before his hungry eyes.

She closed her legs feeling exposed and ashamed but he used his strong hands to pry them apart.

"Trust me," he muttered and she nodded.

She felt a warm breeze down her core. Before she could understand what was going on, he licked her making her squirm. His tongue skillfully sucked and nibbled her core sending her into another wave of pleasure.

He slipped one finger into her and curled it inside of her.

"Lucas," she gasped when he added another finger, thrusting in and out of her.

She couldn't recognize her voice anymore. She sounded so sinful.

"You are so fucking tight, Ariana."

He continued to suck and finger her until she came. She was completely soaked for him.

Her breathing had finally stabilized and she stared down at him "Is that it?" she innocently asked while he laughed.

"That is just the beginning, my dear."

He undid his belt and slipped out of his trousers. Her eyes zeroed on the bulge she could make out through his boxer briefs.

He slipped out of his boxer briefs and she gasped at the huge thing between his legs that was pointing toward her.

He was beautiful in every way, God really had some favorites.

Wasting no time he settled between her thighs, aligning himself against her.

A part of him wondered if he would fit inside her. He could see that the fear in her eyes mirrored his but there was no going back now. They were both ready for this.

"Are you ready?" he asked giving her a chance to make a choice for the both of them.

She nodded confidently and he smiled.

He pushed his tip gently into her and filled her inch by inch until he was completely inside of her.

She gasped and he captured her whimpers with a kiss. He withdrew back and stared at her in concern.

"Are you okay?"

She nodded unable to form words to describe the searing pain she was feeling.

Her insides felt tender. Her body was not used to the feeling.

"I promise to be gentle," he whispered and captured her lips in another kiss and began to move his hips, thrusting in and out of her at a slow pace.

He plunged his fangs into her neck as he fucked her slowly. She screamed from the pain which was soon replaced by overwhelming pleasure. She felt more aroused than never before.

He thrusted into her harder and deeper, losing himself to the pleasure, soon groans and moans filled the room.

She wrapped her hands around his back for support and ended up digging her nails into his skin as he fucked her harder and faster.

Her moans were driving him crazy.

She started to feel an unfamiliar pressure within the core of her walls and started to tremble.

He grunted and increased his pace. He then bit into her neck to complete the mating process. She cried out in pain and pleasure of her orgasm.

Feeling her tighten around him, he pursued his own release and released his seed inside of her, groaning her name.

They let each other ride their pleasure until the end and he gently pulled out of her sensitive body and dropped next to her.

He stared down at the mark he gave her feeling proud and then he licked it, healing her.

"I love you," she declared.

His heart raced at her confession and he wrapped his hands around her pulling the covers over them.

"I love you too, Ariana. You are mine until eternity."

She never expected to fall in love with a vampire or even be mates with one. However, the emotions he had made her feel was out of this world. He completed her. He was heaven sent.

She snuggled deeper in his warmth because there was no place she would rather be than in his arms.

THE END

www.ingramcontent.com/pod-product-compliance
Lightning Source LLC
Chambersburg PA
CBHW060918130726
48001CB00006B/2292